No Peas, Please!

written by
Victoria Athey

illustrated by
Molly Delaney

Amanda likes a lot of things like chicken wings and onion rings.

The only things she doesn't like are her dog's fleas and fat green peas. She always hides them in her cheeks and spits them out when no one peeks.

At dinnertime in her house,
she's as quiet as a mouse.

As the food is passed around,
Amanda's smile turns to a frown.

8

She loves the potatoes and the pork chop, too, but what is in the pink bowl? Ewwww! She sees them on the other side. There's a big fat bowl of peas. OH MY!

There's nothing to them.
They're just green and round.
I bet they taste much worse than
they sound.

Then Grandma
brings over the dish.
All Amanda can do is
wish, "No peas, please.
No peas, please."
Amanda does not
like what she sees.

Doesn't Grandma know the rule?
Peas are gross! They're not cool!

"No thank you, Grandma.
No peas for me. I do not like them.
Can't you see?" One big scoop, and
then another. What to do?
Where is Mother?

Grandma says, "Oh, come on girl.
Peas are great. Give them a whirl."

"Well just this once, I guess, for you," Amanda says and tries a few.

"Yum! Pretty good I must confess.
These peas are great.
They are the best!"

Now every night at the dinner
table, Amanda eats all the peas
she is able. Peas aren't gross
Amanda learned. Isn't it funny
how the story turned?